A HAUNTED
ISLAND

BY

ALGERNON BLACKWOOD

British Library Cataloguing-in-Publication Data
A catalogue record for this book is available from the
British Library

CONTENTS

ALGERNON BLACKWOOD

Algernon Henry Blackwood was born in Shooter's Hill, South East England, in 1869. In his youth he trained as a doctor at Wellington College in Berkshire, and went on to pursue a number of careers, in areas as varied as milk farming, modelling, journalism and violin teaching. In his thirties, Blackwood returned to England from New York, where he had spent a number of years, and began to write stories of the supernatural.

Blackwood was extremely prolific, producing over the course of his life some ten original collections of short stories, fourteen novels, several children's books, and a number of plays. Most of his work was concerned with the ghostly, mythical or occult–themes which Blackwood was attracted to his whole life–and he is regarded as one of the earlier practitioners of 'weird fiction'. Amongst his best known short stories are 'The Wendigo', and 'The Willows'–a work which H. P. Lovecraft called "the finest weird story I have ever read." In 1914, he produced his short story collection *Incredible Adventures*, which leading literary critic S. T. Joshi has said "may be the premier weird collection of this or any other century." Blackwood worked as an undercover agent for Britain during the First World War, and during the 1920s became famous for reading his ghost stories live on BBC radio and television.

After a number of strokes, Blackwood died in old age in Kent, England.

A HAUNTED ISLAND

Algernon Blackwood

The following events occurred on a small island of isolated position in a large Canadian lake, to whose cool waters the inhabitants of Montreal and Toronto flee for rest and recreation in the hot months. It is only to be regretted that events of such peculiar interest to the genuine student of the psychical should be entirely uncorroborated. Such unfortunately, however, is the case.

Our own party of nearly twenty had returned to Montreal that very day, and I was left in solitary possession for a week or two longer, in order to accomplish some important 'reading' for the law which I had foolishly neglected during the summer.

It was late in September, and the big trout and maskinonge were stirring themselves in the depths of the lake and beginning slowly to move up to the surface waters as the north winds and early frosts lowered their temperature. Already the maples were crimson and gold, and the wild laughter of the loons echoed in sheltered bays that never knew their strange cry in the summer.

With a whole island to oneself, a two-storey cottage, a canoe, and only the chipmunks, and the farmer's weekly visit with eggs and bread, to disturb one, the opportunities for hard reading might be very great. It all depends!

The rest of the party had gone off with many warnings to beware of Indians, and not to stay late enough to be the victim of a frost that thinks nothing of forty below zero. After they had gone, the loneliness of the situation made itself unpleasantly felt. There were no other islands within six or seven miles, and though the mainland forests lay a couple of miles behind me, they stretched for a very great distance unbroken by any signs of human habitation. But, though the island was completely deserted and silent, the rocks and trees that had echoed human laughter and voices almost every hour of the day for two months could not fail to retain some memories of it all; and I was not surprised to fancy I heard a shout or a cry as I passed from rock to rock, and more than once to imagine that I heard my own name called aloud.

In the cottage there were six tiny little bedrooms divided from one another by plain unvarnished partitions of pine. A wooden bedstead, a mattress, and a chair, stood in each room, but I only found two mirrors, and one of these was broken.

The boards creaked a good deal as I moved about, and the signs of occupation were so recent that I could hardly believe

I was alone. I half expected to find someone left behind, still trying to crowd into a box more than it would hold. The door of one room was stiff, and refused for a moment to open, and it required very little persuasion to imagine someone was holding the handle on the inside, and that when it opened I should meet a pair of human eyes.

A thorough search of the floor led me to select as my own sleeping quarters a little room with a diminutive balcony over the veranda roof. The room was very small, but the bed was large, and had the best mattress of them all. It was situated directly over the sitting-room where I should live and do my 'reading', and the miniature window looked out to the rising sun. With the exception of a narrow path which led from the front door and veranda through the trees to the boat-landing, the island was densely covered with maples, hemlocks, and cedars. The trees gathered in round the cottage so closely that the slightest wind made the branches scrape the roof and tap the wooden walls. A few moments after sunset the darkness became impenetrable, and ten yards beyond the glare of the lamps that shone through the sitting-room windows–of which there were four–you could not see an inch before your nose, nor move a step without running up against a tree.

The rest of that day I spent moving my belongings from my tent to the sitting-room, taking stock of the contents of the larder, and chopping enough wood for the stove to last me for a week. After that, just before sunset, I went round the island a couple of times in my canoe for precaution's sake. I had never dreamed of doing this before, but when a man is alone he does things that never occur to him when he is one of a large party.

How lonely the island seemed when I landed again! The sun was down, and twilight is unknown in these northern regions. The darkness comes up at once. The canoe safely pulled up and turned over on her face, I groped my way up the little narrow pathway to the veranda. The six lamps were soon burning merrily in the front room; but in the kitchen, where I 'dined', the shadows were so gloomy, and the lamplight was so inadequate, that the stars could be seen peeping through the cracks between the rafters.

I turned in early that night. Though it was calm and there was no wind, the creaking of my bedstead and the musical gurgle of the water over the rocks below were not the only sounds that reached my ears. As I lay awake, the appalling emptiness of the house grew upon me. The corridors and vacant rooms seemed to echo innumerable footsteps, shufflings, the rustle of skirts, and a constant undertone of whispering. When sleep at length overtook me, the breathings and noises, however, passed gently to mingle with the voices of my dreams.

A week passed by, and the 'reading' progressed favourably. On the tenth day of my solitude, a strange thing happened. I awoke after a good night's sleep to find myself possessed with a marked repugnance for my room. The air seemed to stifle me. The more I tried to define the cause of this dislike, the more unreasonable it appeared. There was something about the room that made me afraid. Absurd as it seems, this feeling clung to me obstinately while dressing, and more than once I caught myself shivering, and conscious of an inclination to get out of the room as quickly as possible. The more I tried to laugh it away, the more real it became; and when at last I was dressed, and went out into the passage, and downstairs into the kitchen, it was with feelings of relief, such as I might imagine would accompany one's escape from the presence of a dangerous contagious disease.

While cooking my breakfast, I carefully recalled every night spent in the room, in the hope that I might in some way connect the dislike I now felt with some disagreeable incident that had occurred in it. But the only thing I could recall was one stormy night when I suddenly awoke and heard the boards creaking so loudly in the corridor that I was convinced there were people in the house. So certain was I of this, that I had descended the stairs, gun in hand, only to find the doors and windows securely fastened, and the mice and black-beetles in sole possession of the floor. This was certainly not sufficient to account for the strength of my feelings.

The morning hours I spent in steady reading; and when I

broke off in the middle of the day for a swim and luncheon, I was very much surprised, if not a little alarmed, to find that my dislike for the room had, if anything, grown stronger. Going upstairs to get a book, I experienced the most marked aversion to entering the room, and while within I was conscious all the time of an uncomfortable feeling that was half uneasiness and half apprehension. The result of it was that, instead of reading, I spent the afternoon on the water paddling and fishing, and when I got home about sundown, brought with me half a dozen delicious black bass for the supper-table and the larder.

As sleep was an important matter to me at this time, I had decided that if my aversion to the room was so strongly marked on my return as it had been before, I would move my bed down into the sitting-room, and sleep there. This was, I argued, in no sense a concession to an absurd and fanciful fear, but simply a precaution to ensure a good night's sleep. A bad night involved the loss of the next day's reading–a loss I was not prepared to incur.

I accordingly moved my bed downstairs into a corner of the sitting-room facing the door, and was moreover uncommonly glad when the operation was completed, and the door of the bedroom closed finally upon the shadows, the silence, and the strange *fear* that shared the room with them.

The croaking stroke of the kitchen clock sounded the hour

of eight as I finished washing up my few dishes, and closing the kitchen door behind me, passed into the front room. All the lamps were lit, and their reflectors, which I had polished up during the day, threw a blaze of light into the room.

Outside the night was still and warm. Not a breath of air was stirring; the waves were silent, the trees motionless, and heavy clouds hung like an oppressive curtain over the heavens. The darkness seemed to have rolled up with unusual swiftness, and not the faintest glow of colour remained to show where the sun had set. There was present in the atmosphere that ominous and overwhelming silence which so often precedes the most violent storms.

I sat down to my books with my brain unusually clear, and in my heart the pleasant satisfaction of knowing that five black bass were lying in the ice-house, and that tomorrow morning the old farmer would arrive with fresh bread and eggs. I was soon absorbed in my books.

As the night wore on the silence deepened. Even the chipmunks were still; and the boards of the floors and walls ceased creaking. I read on steadily till, from the gloomy shadows of the kitchen, came the hoarse sound of the clock striking nine. How loud the strokes sounded! They were like blows of a big hammer. I closed one book and opened another, feeling that I was just warming up to my work.

This, however, did not last long. I presently found that I

was reading the same paragraphs over twice, simple paragraphs that did not require such effort. Then I noticed that my mind began to wander to other things, and the effort to recall my thoughts became harder with each digression. Concentration was growing momentarily more difficult. Presently I discovered that I had turned over two pages instead of one, and had not noticed my mistake until I was well down the page. This was becoming serious. What was the disturbing influence? It could not be physical fatigue. On the contrary, my mind was unusually alert, and in a more receptive condition than usual. I made a new and determined effort to read, and for a short time succeeded in giving my whole attention to my subject. But in a very few moments again I found myself leaning back in my chair, staring vacantly into space.

Something was evidently at work in my subconsciousness. There was something I had neglected to do. Perhaps the kitchen door and windows were not fastened. I accordingly went to see, and found that they were! The fire perhaps needed attention. I went in to see, and found that it was all right! I looked at the lamps, went upstairs into every bedroom in turn, and then went round the house, and even into the ice-house. Nothing was wrong; everything was in its place. Yet something *was* wrong! The conviction grew stronger and stronger within me.

When I at length settled down to my books again and

tried to read, I became aware, for the first time, that the room seemed growing cold. Yet the day had been oppressively warm, and evening had brought no relief. The six big lamps, moreover, gave out heat enough to warm the room pleasantly. But a chilliness, that perhaps crept up from the lake, made itself felt in the room, and caused me to get up to close the glass door opening on to the veranda.

For a brief moment I stood looking out at the shaft of light that fell from the windows and shone some little distance down the pathway, and out for a few feet into the lake.

As I looked I saw a canoe glide into the pathway of light, and immediately crossing it, pass out of sight again into the darkness. It was perhaps a hundred feet from the shore, and it moved swiftly.

I was surprised that a canoe should pass the island at that time of night, for all the summer visitors from the other side of the lake had gone home weeks before, and the island was a long way out of any line of water traffic.

My reading from this moment did not make very good progress, for somehow the picture of that canoe, gliding so dimly and swiftly across the narrow track of light on the black waters, silhouetted itself against the background of my mind with singular vividness. It kept coming between my eyes and the printed page. The more I thought about it the more surprised I became. It was of larger build than any I had seen during the past summer months, and was more like the old Indian war canoes with the high curving bows and stern and wide beam. The more I tried to read, the less success attended my efforts; and finally I closed my books and went out on the veranda to walk up and down a bit, and shake the chilliness out of my bones.

The night was perfectly still, and as dark as imaginable. I stumbled down the path to the little landing wharf, where the water made the very faintest of gurgling under the timbers. The sound of a big tree falling in the mainland forest, far across the lake, stirred echoes in the heavy air, like the first guns of a distant night attack. No other sound disturbed the stillness that reigned supreme.

As I stood upon the wharf in the broad splash of light that followed me from the sitting-room windows, I saw another canoe cross the pathway of uncertain light upon the water, and disappear at once into the impenetrable gloom that lay beyond. This time I saw more distinctly than before. It was like the former canoe, a big birch-bark, with high-crested bows and stern and broad beam. It was paddled by two Indians, of whom the one in the stern–the steerer–appeared to be a very large man. I could see this very plainly; and though the second canoe was much nearer the island than the first, I judged that they were both on their way home to the Government Reservation, which was situated some fifteen miles away upon the mainland.

I was wondering in my mind what could possibly bring any Indians down to this part of the lake at such an hour of the night, when a third canoe, of precisely similar build, and also occupied by two Indians, passed silently round the end of the wharf. This time the canoe was very much nearer shore, and it suddenly flashed into my mind that the three canoes were in reality one and the same, and that only one canoe was circling the island!

This was by no means a pleasant reflection, because, if it were the correct solution of the unusual appearance of the three canoes in this lonely part of the lake at so late an hour, the purpose of the two men could only reasonably be considered to be in some way connected with myself. I had never known of the Indians attempting any violence upon the settlers who shared the wild, inhospitable country with them; at the same time, it was not beyond the region of possibility to suppose . . . But then I did not care even to think of such hideous possibilities, and my imagination immediately sought relief in all manner of other solutions to the problem, which indeed came readily enough to my mind, but did not succeed in recommending themselves to my reason.

Meanwhile, by a sort of instinct, I stepped back out of the bright light in which I had hitherto been standing, and waited in the deep shadow of a rock to see if the canoe would again make its appearance. Here I could see, without being seen, and the precaution seemed a wise one.

After less than five minutes the canoe, as I had anticipated, made its fourth appearance. This time it was not twenty yards from the wharf, and I saw that the Indians meant to land. I recognized the two men as those who had passed before, and the steerer was certainly an immense fellow. It was un- questionably the same canoe. There could be no longer any doubt that for some purpose of their own the men had been going round and round the island for some time, waiting for an opportunity to land. I strained my eyes to follow them in the darkness, but the night had completely swallowed them up, and not even the faintest swish of the paddles reached my ears as the Indians plied their long and powerful strokes. The canoe would be round again in a few moments, and this time it was possible that the men might land. It was well to be prepared. I knew nothing of their intentions, and two to one (when the two are big Indians!) late at night on a lonely island was not exactly my idea of pleasant intercourse.

In a corner of the sitting-room, leaning up against the back wall, stood my Marlin rifle, with ten cartridges in the maga- zine and one lying snugly in the greased breech. There was just time to get up to the house and take up a position of defence in that corner. Without an instant's hesitation I ran up to the veranda, carefully picking my way among the trees, so as to avoid being seen in the light. Entering the room, I shut the door leading to the veranda, and as quickly as possible turned out every one of the six lamps. To be in a room so brilliantly lighted, where my every movement could be observed from outside, while I could see nothing but impenetrable darkness at every window, was by all laws of warfare an unnecessary concession to the enemy. And this enemy, if enemy it was to be, was far too wily and dangerous to be granted any such advantages.

I stood in the corner of the room with my back against the wall, and my hand on the cold rifle-barrel. The table, covered with my books, lay between me and the door, but for the first few minutes after the lights were out the darkness was so intense that nothing could be discerned at all. Then, very gradually, the outline of the room became visible, and the framework of the windows began to shape itself dimly before my eyes.

After a few minutes the door (its upper half of glass), and the two windows that looked out upon the front veranda, became specially distinct; and I was glad that this was so, because if the Indians came up to the house I should be able to see their approach, and gather something of their plans. Nor was I mistaken, for there presently came to my ears the peculiar hollow sound of a canoe landing and being carefully dragged up over the rocks. The paddles I distinctly heard being placed underneath, and the silence that ensued thereupon I rightly interpreted to mean that the Indians were stealthily approaching the house . . .

While it would be absurd to claim that I was not alarmed—even frightened—at the gravity of the situation and its possible outcome, I speak the whole truth when I say that I was not overwhelmingly afraid for myself. I was conscious that even at this stage of the night I was passing into a psychical condition in which my sensations seemed no longer normal. Physical fear at no time entered into the nature of my feelings; and though I kept my hand upon my rifle the greater part of the night, I was all the time conscious that its assistance could be of little avail against the terrors that I had to face. More than once I seemed to feel most curiously that I was in no real sense a part of the proceedings, nor actually involved in them, but that I was playing the part of a spectator—a spectator, moreover, on a psychic rather than on a material plane. Many of my sensations that night were too vague for definite description and analysis, but the main feeling that will stay with me to the end of my days is the awful horror of it all, and the miserable sensation that if the strain had lasted a little longer than was actually the case my mind must inevitably have given way.

Meanwhile I stood still in my corner, and waited patiently for what was to come. The house was as still as the grave, but the inarticulate voices of the night sang in my ears, and

I seemed to hear the blood running in my veins and dancing in my pulses.

If the Indians came to the back of the house, they would find the kitchen door and window securely fastened. They could not get in there without making considerable noise, which I was bound to hear. The only mode of getting in was by means of the door that faced me, and I kept my eyes glued on that door without taking them off for the smallest fraction of a second.

My sight adapted itself every minute better to the darkness. I saw the table that nearly filled the room, and left only a narrow passage on each side. I could also make out the straight backs of the wooden chairs pressed up against it, and could even distinguish my papers and inkstand lying on the white oilcloth covering. I thought of the gay faces that had gathered round that table during the summer, and I longed for the sunlight as I had never longed for it before.

Less than three feet to my left the passage-way led to the kitchen, and the stairs leading to the bedrooms above commenced in the passage-way but almost in the sitting-room itself. Through the windows I could see the dim motionless outlines of the trees: not a leaf stirred, not a branch moved.

A few moments of this awful silence, and then I was aware of a soft tread on the boards of the veranda, so stealthy that it seemed an impression directly on my brain rather than upon the nerves of hearing. Immediately afterwards a black figure darkened the glass door, and I perceived that a face was pressed against the upper panes. A shiver ran down my back, and my hair was conscious of a tendency to rise and stand at right angles to my head.

It was the figure of an Indian, broad-shouldered and immense; indeed, the largest figure of a man I have ever seen outside of a circus hall. By some power of light that seemed to generate itself in the brain, I saw the strong dark face with the aquiline nose and high cheekbones flattened against the glass. The direction of the gaze I could not determine; but faint gleams of light as the big eyes rolled round and showed their whites, told me plainly that no corner of the room escaped their searching.

For what seemed fully five minutes the dark figure stood there, with the huge shoulders bent forward so as to bring the head down to the level of the glass; while behind him, though not nearly so large, the shadowy form of the other Indian swayed to and fro like a bent tree. While I waited in an agony of suspense and agitation for their next movement little currents of icy sensation ran up and down my spine and my heart seemed alternately to stop beating and then start off again with terrifying rapidity. They must have heard its thumping and the singing of the blood in my head! Moreover, I was conscious, as I felt a cold stream of perspiration trickle down my face, of a desire to scream, to shout, to bang the walls like a child, to make a noise, or do anything that would relieve the suspense and bring things to a speedy climax.

It was probably this inclination that led me to another discovery, for when I tried to bring my rifle from behind my back to raise it and have it pointed at the door ready to fire, I found that I was powerless to move. The muscles, paralysed by this strange fear, refused to obey the will. Here indeed was a terrifying complication!

*

There was a faint sound of rattling at the brass knob, and the door was pushed open a couple of inches. A pause of a few seconds, and it was pushed open still further. Without a sound of footsteps that was appreciable to my ears, the two figures glided into the room, and the man behind gently closed the door after him.

They were alone with me between the four walls. Could they see me standing there, so still and straight in my corner? Had they, perhaps, already seen me? My blood surged and sang like the roll of drums in an orchestra; and though I did my best to suppress my breathing, it sounded like the rushing of wind through a pneumatic tube.

My suspense as to the next move was soon at an end—only, however, to give place to a new and keener alarm. The men had hitherto exchanged no words and no signs, but there were general indications of a movement across the room, and whichever way they went they would have to pass round the table. If they came my way they would have to pass within six inches of my person. While I was considering this very disagreeable possibility, I perceived that the smaller Indian (smaller by comparison) suddenly raised his arm and pointed to the ceiling. The other fellow raised his head and followed the direction of his companion's arm. I began to understand at last. They were going upstairs, and the room directly overhead to which they pointed had been until this night my bedroom. It was the room in which I had experienced that very morning so strange a sensation of fear, and but for which I should then have been lying asleep in the narrow bed against the window.

The Indians then began to move silently around the room; they were going upstairs, and they were coming round my side of the table. So stealthy were their movements that, but for the abnormally sensitive state of the nerves, I should never have heard them. As it was, their cat-like tread was distinctly audible. Like two monstrous black cats they came round the table towards me, and for the first time I perceived that the smaller of the two dragged something along the floor behind him. As it trailed along over the floor with a soft, sweeping sound, I somehow got the impression that it was a large dead thing with outstretched wings, or a large, spreading cedar branch. Whatever it was, I was unable to see it even in out-line, and I was too terrified, even had I possessed the power over my muscles, to move my neck forward in the effort to determine its nature.

Nearer and nearer they came. The leader rested a giant hand upon the table as he moved. My lips were glued together, and the air seemed to burn in my nostrils. I tried to close my eyes, so that I might not see as they passed me; but my eyelids had stiffened, and refused to obey. Would they never get by me? Sensation seemed also to have left my legs, and it was as if I were standing on mere supports of wood or stone. Worse still, I was conscious that I was losing the power of balance, the power to stand upright, or even to lean backwards against the wall. Some force was drawing me forward, and a dizzy terror seized me that I should lose my balance, and topple forward against the Indians just as they were in the act of passing me.

Even moments drawn out into hours must come to an end some time, and almost before I knew it the figures had passed me and had their feet upon the lower step of the stairs leading to the upper bedrooms. There could not have been six inches between us, and yet I was conscious only of a current of cold air that followed them. They had not touched me, and I was convinced that they had not seen me. Even the trailing thing on the floor behind them had not touched my feet, as I had dreaded it would, and on such an occasion as this I was grateful even for the smallest mercies.

The absence of the Indians from my immediate neighbourhood brought little sense of relief. I stood shivering and shuddering in my corner, and, beyond being able to breathe more freely, I felt no whit less uncomfortable. Also, I was aware that a certain light, which, without apparent source or rays, had enabled me to follow their every gesture and movement, had gone out of the room with their departure. An unnatural darkness now filled the room, and pervaded its every corner so that I could barely make out the positions of the windows and the glass doors.

As I said before, my condition was evidently an abnormal one. The capacity for feeling surprise seemed, as in dreams, to be wholly absent. My senses recorded with unusual accuracy every smallest occurrence, but I was able to draw only the simplest deductions.

The Indians soon reached the top of the stairs, and there they halted for a moment. I had not the faintest clue as to their next movement. They appeared to hesitate. They were listening attentively. Then I heard one of them, who by the weight of his soft tread must have been the giant, cross the narrow corridor and enter the room directly overhead–my own little bedroom. But for the insistence of that unaccountable dread I had experienced there in the morning, I should at that very moment have been lying in the bed with the big Indian in the room standing beside me.

For a space of a hundred seconds there was silence, such as

might have existed before the birth of sound. It was followed by a long quivering shriek of terror, which rang out into the night, and ended in a short gulp before it had run its full course. At the same moment the other Indian left his place at the head of the stairs, and joined his companion in the bedroom. I heard the 'thing' trailing behind him along the floor. A thud followed, as of something heavy falling, and then all became as still and silent as before.

It was at this point that the atmosphere, surcharged all day with the electricity of a fierce storm, found relief in a dancing flash of brilliant lightning simultaneously with a crash of loudest thunder. For five seconds every article in the room was visible to me with amazing distinctness, and through the windows I saw the tree trunks standing in solemn rows. The thunder pealed and echoed across the lake and among the distant islands, and the flood-gates of heaven then opened and let out their rain in streaming torrents.

The drops fell with a swift rushing sound upon the still waters of the lake, which leaped up to meet them, and pattered with the rattle of shot on the leaves of the maples and the roof of the cottage. A moment later, and another flash, even more brilliant and of longer duration than the first, lit up the sky from zenith to horizon, and bathed the room momentarily in dazzling whiteness. I could see the rain glistening on the leaves and branches outside. The wind rose suddenly, and in less than a minute the storm that had been gathering all day burst forth in its full fury.

Above all the noisy voices of the elements, the slightest sounds in the room overhead made themselves heard, and in the few seconds of deep silence that followed the shriek of terror and pain I was aware that the movements had commenced again. The men were leaving the room and approaching the top of the stairs. A short pause, and they began to descend. Behind them, tumbling from step to step, I could hear that trailing 'thing' being dragged along. It had become ponderous!

I awaited their approach with a degree of calmness, almost of apathy, which was only explicable on the ground that after a certain point Nature applies her own anaesthetic, and a merciful condition of numbness supervenes. On they came, step by step, nearer and nearer, with the shuffling sound of the burden behind growing louder as they approached.

They were already half-way down the stairs when I was galvanized afresh into a condition of terror by the consideration of a new and horrible possibility. It was the reflection that if another vivid flash of lightning were to come when the shadowy procession was in the room, perhaps when it was actually passing in front of me, I should see everything in detail, and worse, be seen myself! I could only hold my breath and wait—wait while the minutes lengthened into hours, and the procession made its slow progress round the room.

The Indians had reached the foot of the staircase. The form of the huge leader loomed in the doorway of the passage, and the burden with an ominous thud had dropped from the last step to the floor. There was a moment's pause while I saw the Indian turn and stoop to assist his companion. Then the procession moved forward again, entered the room close on my left, and began to move slowly round my side of the table. The leader was already beyond me, and his companion, dragging on the floor behind him the burden, whose confused outline I could dimly make out, was exactly in front of me, when the cavalcade came to a dead halt. At the same moment, with the strange suddenness of thunderstorms, the splash of the rain ceased altogether, and the wind died away into utter silence.

For the space of five seconds my heart seemed to stop beating, and then the worst came. A double flash of lightning lit up the room and its contents with merciless vividness.

The huge Indian leader stood a few feet past me on my right. One leg was stretched forward in the act of taking a step. His immense shoulders were turned towards his companion, and in all their magnificent fierceness I saw the outline of his features. His gaze was directed upon the burden his companion was dragging along the floor; but his profile, with the big aquiline nose, high cheekbone, straight black hair and bold chin, burnt itself in that brief instant into my brain, never again to fade.

Dwarfish, compared with this gigantic figure, appeared the proportions of the other Indian, who, within twelve inches of my face, was stooping over the thing he was dragging in a position that lent to his person the additional horror of deformity. And the burden, lying upon a sweeping cedar branch which he held and dragged by a long stem, was the body of a white man. The scalp had been neatly lifted, and blood lay in a broad smear upon the cheeks and forehead.

Then, for the first time that night, the terror that had paralysed my muscles and my will lifted its unholy spell from my soul. With a loud cry I stretched out my arms to seize the big Indian by the throat, and, grasping only air, tumbled forward unconscious upon the ground.

I had recognized the body, and *the face was my own!* . . .

It was bright daylight when a man's voice recalled me to consciousness. I was lying where I had fallen, and the farmer was standing in the room with the loaves of bread in his hands. The horror of the night was still in my heart, and as the bluff settler helped me to my feet and picked up the rifle which had fallen with me, with many questions and expressions of condolence, I imagine my brief replies were neither self-explanatory nor even intelligible.

That day, after a thorough and fruitless search of the house, I left the island, and went over to spend my last ten days with the farmer; and when the time came for me to leave, the necessary reading had been accomplished, and my nerves had completely recovered their balance.

On the day of my departure the farmer started early in his big boat with my belongings to row to the point, twelve miles distant, where a little steamer ran twice a week for the accommodation of hunters. Late in the afternoon I went off in another direction in my canoe, wishing to see the island once again, where I had been the victim of so strange an experience.

In due course I arrived there, and made a tour of the island. I also made a search of the little house, and it was not without a curious sensation in my heart that I entered the little upstairs bedroom. There seemed nothing unusual.

Just after I re-embarked, I saw a canoe gliding ahead of me around the curve of the island. A canoe was an unusual sight at this time of the year, and this one seemed to have sprung from nowhere. Altering my course a little, I watched it disappear around the next projecting point of rock. It had high curving bows, and there were two Indians in it. I lingered with some excitement, to see if it would appear again round the other side of the island; and in less than five minutes it came into view. There were less than two hundred yards between us, and the Indians, sitting on their haunches, were paddling swiftly in my direction.

I never paddled faster in my life than I did in those next few minutes. When I turned to look again, the Indians had altered their course, and were again circling the island.

The sun was sinking behind the forests on the mainland, and the crimson-coloured clouds of sunset were reflected in the waters of the lake, when I looked round for the last time, and saw the big bark canoe and its two dusky occupants still going round the island. Then the shadows deepened rapidly; the lake grew black, and the night wind blew its first breath in my face as I turned a corner, and a projecting bluff of rock hid from my view both island and canoe.